Peppa Pig™

The Fancy Dress Party

Peppa and George are
having a fancy dress party.
All their friends are invited.

Peppa is dressed as
a fairy princess and
George is a dinosaur.

All the guests are arriving.
Rebecca Rabbit is dressed as a carrot
and Suzy Sheep has come as a nurse.
"Hello, Suzy," says Daddy Pig. "Have
you just come from the hospital?"

"I'm not a real nurse,"
says Suzy Sheep.
"It's just pretend."

"Hello, Suzy," says Peppa. "I'm Princess Peppa.
You must bow when you speak to me."
Suzy Sheep bows.

"Woof! Woof!
I'm a pirate!
Shiver me timbers!"
says Danny Dog.

"Neigh! I'm a clown," says Pedro, tooting his horn.
"Rebecca, why are you dressed as a carrot?"
Danny asks.

"Because I like carrots," says Rebecca.
George does his best dinosaur roar
and scares everybody.

Peppa is playing by herself. She pretends the mirror is magic. "Mirror, mirror, on the wall, who is the fairest of them all . . . ? You are, Peppa!" she giggles.

It's time to judge the fancy dress competition.
"As it's Peppa's party," says Daddy Pig,
"she can be the judge and decide who has
the best costume."

The guests show off their outfits.
"I'm a pirate. Shiver me timbers!" says Danny Dog.
"I'm a nurse who makes people better," says Suzy Sheep.

Candy Cat
waves her wand
at Peppa.
"I'm a witch, and
I can turn you
into a frog,"
she says.

"Well, I'm a fairy princess and I can turn you into a frog," cries Peppa.

It is time to announce the winner. "Everyone's costume is very good," says Peppa. "But the winner is . . . me!"

"Peppa, you can't pick yourself, you're the judge!" whispers Mummy Pig.
"Oh! Can't I?" asks Peppa.
"You have to pick another winner," Mummy Pig says quietly.

"OK, the carrot wins," says Peppa.
Hooray! Rebecca Rabbit has won the
fancy dress competition.
"Thank you," Rebecca says.

Peppa loves fancy dress parties.
Everyone loves fancy dress parties!